The Adventures of Cray on the Bay

BEACH BALL BLUNDER

Written by G Pa Rhymes &
Illustrated by Erica Leigh

G Pa Rhymes

Illustrations by Erica Leigh: www.EricaLeighArt.com
Edited by Erica Leigh

First hardcover edition; November 2021
ISBN   978-1-7348031-3-6
G Pa Rhymes Publishing
GPaRhymes.com

To my mother, Marilyn Harter, a retired Professor of English Literature. Her students consistently named her their favorite professor, and before she was their teacher, she was mine.

To my "dad" Russell Harter, whose love, support, and advice have been a true blessing in my life.

I love you both very much!

Your son,

~G PA RHYMES

The sunrise was spectacular
and colors filled the sky.
When Cray was with his friends,
he was a very happy guy.

Sitting on the jetty rocks
their clever friend, Seal Gray,
was spinning beach balls on his nose—
his favorite way to play.

The ball was spinning faster,
Gray delighted with a grin.
He bounced and bounced, not knowing,
soon the trouble would begin.

It shot way up into the air
and almost hit Gull Ray.

It plummeted back toward the beach
then bounced off Turtle Fay.

A rebound on the sand dune
sent it zooming to the beach.

Cray stretched out to stop the ball,
too bad he couldn't reach.

Then straight into an ice cream cone,
half-eaten by a girl,

that beach ball splattered everything
with double rainbow swirl!

Fox Hay kept both eyes covered
when the ball came rolling by.
Her sandcastle was flattened
and it made her want to cry.

Gray was feeling guilty,
scared of what his friends might say.
He told a lie to make
that awful feeling go away.

When eyes were turned upon him
Gray exclaimed, "It wasn't me!
It must have come from somewhere else,
did anybody see?"

What an awful situation!
They were getting so upset,
saying mean things to each other,
hurtful words they would regret.

Sadness grew within Gray's heart,
his body filled with fright.
Scared to tell the truth,
he knew he had to make it right.

"Please, let's stop our fighting.
It was me—it was *my* ball.
I'm sorry that I lied,
that I upset and hurt you all!"

Cray explained that lying
only causes lots of harm.

"Accidents will happen
like that time I lost my arm."

Gray said, "I've learned my lesson
and I'll never lie again."
He worked all afternoon
to clean the mess and help his friends.

"We forgive you Gray," said Cray,
"that's what good friends do.
Now let's all go and have some fun.
We'd love to play with you!"

Cray was sure his group of friends
could handle anything.

He cracked a smile and wondered
what the coming day would bring.

Have you read the first two books in the series?
"The Adventures of Cray on the Bay"

A New Day for Cray

After an unfortunate accident, Cray learns how a good friend should make you feel.

Cray Saves the Day

Turtle Fay is in a bind, and with the help of Queen Mer May, Cray and his friends work together to make the beach a safer place for all.

After you've read this book
please write a review.
G Pa and Erica appreciate you!